THE COLD WAR CHRONICLES

The Collapse of Communism and the Breakup of the Soviet Union

Cathleen Small

Cavendish Square
New York

Published in 2018 by Cavendish Square Publishing, LLC
243 5th Avenue, Suite 136, New York, NY 10016

First Edition

CPSIA Compliance Information: Batch #CS17CSQ

All websites were available and accurate when this book was sent to press.

Library of Congress Cataloging-in-Publication Data

Names: Small, Cathleen, author.
Title: The collapse of communism and the break up of the Soviet Union / Cathleen Small.
Description: New York : Cavendish Square Publishing, [2018] | Series: The Cold War chronicles | Includes bibliographical references and index.
Identifiers: LCCN 2016058847 (print) | LCCN 2017000067 (ebook) | ISBN 9781502627285 (library bound) | ISBN 9781502627261 (E-book)
Subjects: LCSH: Soviet Union--Politics and government--1985-1991--Juvenile literature. | Communist countries--Politics and government--Juvenile literature. | Cold War--Juvenile literature.
Classification: LCC DK288 .S586 2018 (print) | LCC DK288 (ebook) | DDC 947.085/4--dc23
LC record available at https://lccn.loc.gov/2016058847

Editorial Director: David McNamara
Editor: Jodyanne Benson
Copy Editor: Rebecca Rohan
Associate Art Director: Amy Greenan
Designer: Alan Sliwinski
Production Coordinator: Karol Szymczuk
Photo Research: J8 Media

The photographs in this book are used by permission and through the courtesy of: Cover Gerard Malie/AFP/Getty Images; p. 4 SVF2/Universal Images Group/Getty Images; p. 8 Sovfoto/Universal Images Group/Getty Images; pp. 11, 16, 58 Bettmann/Getty Images; p. 12 Library of Congress/Corbis Historical/Getty Images; p. 19 Corbis Historical/ Getty Images; p. 20 David Hume Kennerly/Archive Photos/Getty Images; p. 23 Dick Swanson/The LIFE Images Collection/Getty Images; p. 26 Anatoly Sapronenko/AFP/Getty Images; p. 28 Wikimedia Commons/File:USSR Republics Numbered Alphabetically.png/CC BY-SA 3.0; p. 30 Alphathon/File:Military power of NATO and the Warsaw Pact states in 1973.svg/CC BY-SA 3.0; p. 32 Kommersant Photo/Getty Images; p. 36 James Whitmore/The LIFE Picture Collection/Getty Images; pp. 39, 84 AP Images; p. 47 TASS/Getty Images; p. 50 Wikimedia Commons/ File:Joseph Stalin and Nikita Khrushchev,1936.jpg/CCO; p. 53 Wikimedia Commons/File:Stalin-Joseph-1930.jpg/ CCO; p. 62 Sovfoto/Universal Images Group/Getty Images; p. 66 SVF2/Universal Images Group/Getty Images; p. 70 Hector Mata/AFP/Getty Images; p. 72 Imgorthand/E+/Getty Images; p. 75 Aunt Spray/iStock/Thinkstock; p. 76 Mark Stevenson/Stocktrek Images/Getty Images; p. 80 NASA/The LIFE Picture Collection/Getty Images; p. 83 MarcelClemens/Shutterstock.com; p. 88 Anadolu Agency/Getty Images; p. 90 Jewel Samad/Getty Images; p. 92 Alexander Nemenov/AFP/Getty Images; p. 94 Hanout/Getty Images; p. 96 Gerard Malie/AFP/Getty Images.

Printed in the United States of America

CONTENTS

SS-4 missiles on display at a 1961 Moscow parade

The Mighty Fall that Led to the End of the Cold War

The Cold War took place from about 1945 to about 1991. Exact dates are difficult to establish because the Cold War was not a physical conflict in which one country declared war on another. There was no invasion, and no truce was signed. Rather, the Cold War was a time of prolonged tension between the world's two superpowers—the United States and the Soviet Union.

During World War II, the United States and the Soviet Union had fought Germany as allies. However, when the Nazis were defeated and the war ended, it came time to divide up formerly Nazi-occupied territories. The United States ended up overseeing much of Western Europe, while the Soviet Union took most of Eastern Europe. German was split into two—Allied West Germany and Soviet East Germany—and Berlin (the capital of Germany) itself was split into multiple zones of occupation. This division of countries and territories led to what was known as the Western Bloc and the Eastern Bloc. The Western Bloc, more commonly known as the free world or the Western world, was made up of countries allied with the United States and other NATO countries, and the Eastern Bloc was made up of countries allied with the Soviet Union, such as Poland, Romania, and Bulgaria.

The two superpowers had very different economic and government systems. The United States was a capitalist, democratic system, whereas the Soviet Union was a one-party Communist nation with a largely socialist economy. Because the philosophies were so different, it resulted in the two superpowers constantly jockeying to ensure that the other nation didn't gain too much in power. The Soviets wanted to maintain their power and, in theory, ally with other Communist nations, while the United States and its allies feared the spread of Communism.

These tensions resulted in decades of tense relationships and political maneuvering as well as proxy wars, numerous conflicts, and a race to surpass each other in space and weapons technology. Throughout it all, the threat of nuclear war loomed. Both the United States and the Soviet Union had developed nuclear weapons technology and could, in theory, unleash it at any time. Over the decades of the Cold War, what kept all-out nuclear war from breaking out was largely the doctrine of mutually assured destruction (MAD)—both superpowers knew that if they unleashed nuclear weapons, it would be certain destruction of *both* nations.

Ultimately, what resolved these tensions was the end of the Cold War, which came about due to the fall of the Soviet Union. When the Soviet Union collapsed, there was suddenly only one world superpower, the United States, and thus the threat of global war between two superpowers largely dissolved.

The Cold War spanned many decades, and although the fall of the Soviet Union largely took place over the span of about six years, the fractures that precipitated the fall were a long time coming. Many leaders were part of the ongoing Cold War tensions that ultimately resulted in the surprising and spectacular crash of the once-mighty Soviet Union. Some of these faces were Americans: Presidents Harry S. Truman, John F. Kennedy, and Ronald Reagan, for example. Others were Soviet leaders, such as Joseph Stalin, Nikita Khrushchev, and Mikhail Gorbachev. Still others were a bit more on the periphery, such as Cuban Communist leader Fidel Castro, who figured prominently in the Cuban Missile Crisis, a defining event of the Cold War.

The faces and events of the Cold War are many, but the faces and events specifically related to the fall of the Soviet Union weave a fascinating piece of history.

Surface-to-air missiles at
a 1957 Moscow parade

CHAPTER ONE

Mounting Tensions

The collapse of Communism and the breakup of the Soviet Union generally marked the end of the Cold War. The Cold War wasn't a traditional military conflict with concrete start and end dates, but certainly there are important events that occurred over those decades and marked the mounting tensions that eventually led to the dissolution of the Soviet Union and its collapse as a Communist nation.

Allies Turned Adversaries

Although the United States and the Soviet Union had two distinct government systems (a democracy and a Communist system, respectively), the two superpowers were allies during World War II as they fought against Nazi forces in Germany and other European countries. They had a common goal, after all: Hitler's armies were spreading far and fast in

Europe, including into the Soviet Union, and neither wanted to see a global Nazi takeover.

But after the war was over, the alliance between the two nations dissolved, and familiar disagreements emerged. The United States, which occupied Western Europe with Great Britain and France at the end of the war, did not support Communism and thus actively worked to stem the spread of Soviet influence in Western Europe—and later, worldwide. Meanwhile, the Soviet Union established Communist regimes in Eastern European countries it occupied after the war, including Poland, Hungary, Bulgaria, Czechoslovakia (now the Czech Republic), Romania, Albania, and East Germany.

And so began a long, uneasy period of relations between the United States and the Soviet Union, filled with tense political maneuvering, military actions, and proxy wars.

Kicking Off the Cold War: The Truman Doctrine and the Marshall Plan

Although there is no exact beginning to the Cold War, it began after the end of World War II and is often thought to have taken shape in about 1947, on the heels of the Truman Doctrine and the Marshall Plan.

The Truman Doctrine provided aid to governments that were in danger of falling to Communism. In March 1947, United States president Harry S. Truman proposed the doctrine to Congress. He was concerned about the spread of Communism and what it could mean for the United

Truman proposed the Truman Doctrine before Congress in March 1947.

States. If nations were vulnerable to Communist influence and takeover and began falling to Communism, the power of Communism would only continue to grow and would eventually pose a threat to national security as well as to world peace.

The Conflict of Communism and Capitalism

Anti-Communist posters such as this one were common during the Cold War.

So why did the United States consider the Soviet Union such a threat? A large part of the answer is that the political and economic systems of the countries were so different. The Soviet Union was a Communist nation, while the United States was a federal republic with a capitalist economy, and many of the rights that Americans have under their system would have been lost under a Communist system.

You might see the terms socialism and Communism used interchangeably when someone is referring to the Soviet system. (Note that the Soviet Union, run by the Communist Party, was technically named the Union of Soviet Socialist Republics, or USSR.) Technically, socialism is an economic system, while Communism is an economic and political system. Both systems emphasize removing the class hierarchies that exist in a capitalist society. Some describe socialism as a step on the road to the more radical Communism—in other words, a nation would first develop a socialist economy and then might continue toward the fully classless society envisioned by proponents of Communism. The Soviet Union tried to accomplish this through a one-party system that included a centrally planned economy, curbing of religion, heavy government surveillance, and a sizeable military.

It might be easy to see how Communism is in direct contrast to capitalism, which is based on individual rights and individual ownership of property. While socialist and Communist systems believe in a common good and a lack of class hierarchy, a capitalist society recognizes that each individual works for his or her own common good and that class divisions are inherent in a free market.

Of course, there are various types and subsets of each type of system (for example, **Marxist** Communism, democratic socialism, and laissez-faire capitalism), but the important takeaway is that Communism and capitalism were the two main political systems at play during the Cold War, and the United States considered Communism a tremendous threat.

Truman's plan wasn't a particularly tough sell. Americans had just seen the horrors of what happened as countries fell to a nondemocratic model of government (the Nazi Party) and were understandably wary of any sort of government takeover that even remotely resembled the totalitarian ideals behind the Nazi Party. Truman's impassioned speech to Congress, delivered on March 12, 1947, insisted that "it must be the policy of the United States to support free peoples who are resisting attempted subjugation by armed minorities and by outside pressures." He further stated that "we must assist free peoples to work out their own destinies in their own way" and "our help should be primarily through economic and financial aid which is essential to economic stability and orderly political processes." In other words, support free nations so they can achieve political stability rather than fall to Communism.

The initial thrust of the Truman Doctrine was directed toward preventing a Communist takeover of Greece and Turkey by the Soviet Union, but the doctrine was later applied to other nations that were under threat of Communist takeover as well. In fact, it became a bedrock of United States foreign policy during the Cold War and beyond. And ultimately, it led to the formation of the North Atlantic Treaty Organization (NATO) in 1949. NATO basically ensured that member nations would mount a united, mutual defense if one of those nations were attacked by a non-NATO nation. This alliance became very important as the Cold War progressed and the United States and other non-Communist nations fought to stem the spread of Communism.

On a similar note, the Marshall Plan provided economic assistance to countries with unstable, democratically elected government structures that would otherwise be ripe for Communist takeover. Over a period of four years, the United States gave Western European nations more than twelve billion dollars to help them rebuild their economies and ensure political stability in those nations. Perhaps not surprisingly given their political disagreement with the United States, the Soviet Union refused to accept any aid from the Marshall Plan and would not allow countries in the Eastern Bloc to accept any either.

The Berlin Blockade and the Berlin Wall

Another factor in the mounting tensions during the early years of the Cold War was the Berlin Blockade, which took place over a period of ten months starting in June 1948. After World War II, Germany had been divided into four temporary occupation zones. These were divided into Allied territory (controlled by the United States, Great Britain, and France) in West Germany and Soviet-controlled territory in East Germany. Berlin, the capital of Germany, was actually divided into Allies-controlled and Soviet-controlled sections, although the city itself lay well inside East Germany. As the Soviets established the Socialist Unity Party (*Sozialistische Einheitspartei Deutschlands*, or SED) in East Germany, the Allies worked to support a new, non-Communist political system in West Germany. The citizens of divided Berlin

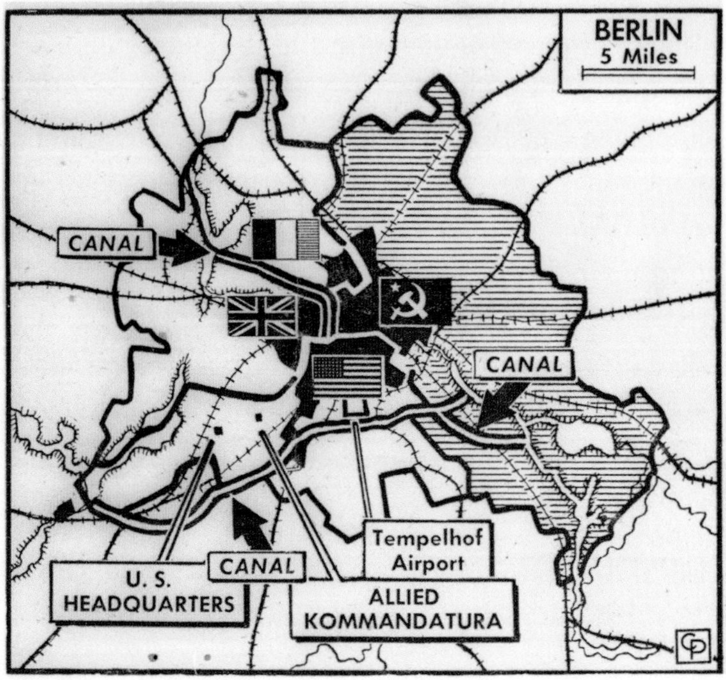

The Soviets established the Berlin Blockade to thwart the Allies, but the Allies were able to transport needed supplies to the region by air.

did not want to be part of a Communist political system, but they were geographically located in the heart of the Soviet-controlled region.

Therefore, Berlin became a battleground in the escalating tensions. The Soviet Union blocked rail, road, and boat access to the portions of Berlin that the Allies controlled to prevent the Allies from getting supplies to the citizens there. However, the Allies recognized and exploited a loophole in the blockade—the Soviets had not stopped air traffic into the region—and the Allies were able to get supplies to the people of West Berlin by airplane.

The Allies were successful in delivering supplies by air, and the Soviets didn't fight this because they did not want to incite outright conflict: stopping flights into West Berlin could lead to war with the Allies, and the Soviets weren't ready to go that far. Eventually, they dropped the blockade when they realized the Allies had succeeded in circumventing it.

The tensions didn't end in Berlin, though. More than a decade later, East Germany (known as the German Democratic Republic, or GDR—a rather ironic name, given that it described the Communist half of the country) constructed the Berlin Wall. The wall was a physical barrier between West Berlin and East Berlin and the rest of East Germany. The Eastern Bloc built the wall to prevent citizens from East Germany from leaving the Communist region, though they claimed it was to prevent NATO members in Western Europe—in particular, West Germany—from discouraging East German citizens to build a socialist state.

The Berlin Wall was essentially impenetrable to East German citizens until 1989, when crossing restrictions were lifted as Communist governments in the region began to falter and crumble. Physically, the wall stood until 1992, but demolition began in 1990.

Proxy Wars

The Cold War itself was never a conflict in which the United States and the Soviet Union battled each other physically. However, the Cold War did include numerous proxy wars that involved direct support from the Soviet Union and the United States. Because a direct conflict between the United States and the Soviet Union could have resulted in nuclear war, the two superpowers instead asserted themselves politically by supporting these proxy wars. Certain conflicts of the Cold War, such as the Berlin Blockade and the Cuban Missile Crisis, were technically considered proxy wars. But other proxy wars were more of what we consider traditionally to be wars—conflicts with physical fighting by military forces. Two of the most notable of the era were the Korean War and the Vietnam War.

The Korean War

The Korean War took place from 1950 to 1953, and at its most basic level, it was a fight between Communist North Korea and democratic South Korea. On June 25, 1950, North Korea invaded South Korea in an attempted Communist takeover, which started the war. However, the Soviet Union and the United States both figured prominently in this war. The Soviet Union (along with other Eastern Bloc countries and Communist China) gave support in the form of pilots and military aircraft, weapons, tanks, and medical services to Communist North Korea, while the United States (and other members of the United Nations) supported South Korea.

This division actually went back to the end of World War II, when Korea was divided at the thirty-eighth parallel, with the Soviet Union liberating the north and the United States stationing forces in the south. It was an uneasy sort of truce, with two separate governments running the two halves of the country until North Korea invaded South Korea. When North Korea invaded South Korea, the United Nations stepped in to defend South Korea, and part of that defense included the United States stationing a large number of military personnel to aid in the fight. The United States was keen to protect South Korea in part because of its proximity to Japan. China had fallen to Communist rule, and the United States wanted Japan to remain a non-Communist nation. Thus, it was important that South Korea not fall to

US soldiers took Chinese Red Army soldiers prisoner during the Korean War.

Fidel Castro: Friend to the Soviets

Fidel Castro ruled Cuba for forty-seven years, first as prime minister and then as president. Although part of the Communist Party of Cuba, his political ideology was actually Marxist-Leninist, and Cuba was a socialist state under his rule. Castro was instrumental in overthrowing Cuban president Fulgencio Batista and installing himself as Cuban prime minister in the wake of the overthrow.

The United States did not support Castro's rule of Cuba. In fact, the Central Intelligence Agency (CIA) attempted to assassinate him on multiple occasions under multiple presidential administrations, and they attempted to overthrow him in the failed Bay of Pigs

Fidel Castro was an oppressive leader of Cuba for nearly fifty years.

invasion. They also enacted an embargo against trade with Cuba. In short, the United States made their distaste for Castro's leadership abundantly clear.

Castro reacted in part by forming an alliance with the United States' enemy—the Soviet Union. He allowed the Soviets to place nuclear weapons in Cuba, and he ruled Cuba as the first pro-Soviet socialist state in the Western Hemisphere. This was very troubling to the United States, which had fought for more than a decade to prevent the spread of Communism in the East—and now here it was in the West, less than a hundred miles from United States land.

Castro's strong ties with the Soviet Union existed until the mid-1980s, when Mikhail Gorbachev assumed leadership in the Soviet Union. Gorbachev made a number of reforms to the Soviet politics and economy, including increasing freedom of the press and restructuring the economic system—changes Castro did not agree with and did not implement in Cuba. Further, Gorbachev and United States president Ronald Reagan engaged in talks that led to Gorbachev agreeing to reduce Soviet support of Cuba. In 1989, Gorbachev informed Castro that the Soviet Union would no longer provide Cuba with subsidies.

When Castro became ill and unable to rule Cuba, he transferred rule to his vice president—who happened to be his brother, Raúl Castro. Although Raúl Castro is slightly more moderate than his brother Fidel, he is still a member of the Communist Party, and Cuba remains a Communist state. Fidel Castro died at the age of ninety on November 26, 2016.

Communism. In total, more than five million United States troops fought in Korea.

The United States' decision to support South Korea was due to the domino theory that President Truman had defined in his speech about the Truman Doctrine—the idea that if one country fell to Communism, then a neighboring country might, then another, in a chain reaction that would eventually topple democracy and could result in a worldwide Communist takeover. While the Soviet Union wanted to maintain a Communist foothold in the region, the United States wanted just the opposite.

Technically, although the Korean War ended in 1953, there was no peace treaty signed. The two halves of the country remain in conflict with each other, with separate government structures.

The Vietnam War

The Vietnam War was another major proxy war of the Cold War era. In some ways, it was similar to the Korean War. Vietnam was divided into two halves—North Vietnam and South Vietnam. North Vietnam was under Communist rule and sought to overtake South Vietnam. In response, the United States sent troops and aid to South Vietnam to help them in their fight against Communist takeover. The Soviet Union, not surprisingly, supported North Vietnam in the war and provided economic and material support. They did not, however, enter the conflict directly by sending troops to fight.

The motivations were similar to those during the Korean War. The Soviet Union was in favor of Communist rule in the region, whereas the United States feared that allowing South Vietnam to fall to Communism would be a blow to the United States' attempt to stem Communist takeover. Unlike the Korean War, the Vietnam War resulted in one side "winning." After many years of conflict, South Vietnam fell to North Vietnam in 1975—a victory for the Soviet Union, even if not directly.

Perhaps the largest proxy war during the Cold War was the Vietnam conflict, which was not *technically* a war, though it is generally referred to as such.

The Cuban Missile Crisis

Although the Cuban Missile Crisis is technically considered a proxy war, it was more of a thirteen-day standoff between the United States and the Soviet Union. It was, however, terrifying because it could have erupted into a full-scale nuclear war.

The United States had attempted to overthrow the Communist regime of Fidel Castro by mounting the Bay of Pigs invasion on April 17, 1961. However, the mission failed when Cuban armed forces defeated the Brigade 2506 paramilitary group that undertook the invasion. Castro had strong ties to the Soviet Union, and given Cuba's location just ninety miles off the coast of Florida, President Eisenhower and the United States government were greatly concerned about the Soviet influence in Castro's Cuba.

When the United States invaded Cuba (albeit unsuccessfully), it put the Soviet Union on the defensive. After all, the United States had missiles in Italy and Turkey, which were dangerously close to the Soviet Union. So, in 1962, Soviet leader Nikita Khrushchev agreed to put nuclear weapons in Cuba.

When the United States received credible evidence that the Soviet Union had indeed placed nuclear missiles in Cuba, they demanded that the missiles be removed and that no further such weapons be placed in Cuba. There was a lot of tension for nearly two weeks while President John F. Kennedy (who took office in 1962) negotiated with Khrushchev about the missiles. Americans lived in fear of whether the missiles in Cuba, so close to United States soil, would be deployed. Eventually, Kennedy and Khrushchev reached an agreement, and the Soviets removed the missiles from Cuba while the United States publicly agreed not to invade Cuba unless they were directly provoked. And although the United States missiles in Italy and Turkey were not subject to public knowledge, the United States agreed to remove them.

Cold War Tensions Boil Over

The Cold War was full of many events and conflicts that contributed to the mounting tension between the United States and the Soviet Union and the eventual crumbling of the latter. When the Soviet Union finally dissolved, it marked the end of the nearly fifty-year war.

Soviet tanks occupy the area near the entrance of the Kremlin in 1991, shortly after a failed coup to overthrow Mikhail Gorbachev.

CHAPTER TWO

The Collapse of Communism and the Breakup of the Soviet Union

While the mounting tensions in the decades of the Cold War largely involved multiple conflicts between the world's two superpowers, the United States and the Soviet Union, the actual breakdown of Communism and ultimate fall of the Soviet Union had more to do with internal fracturing of the Soviet political and economic structure. Certainly, the United States was a presence, as President Ronald Reagan and Soviet leader Mikhail Gorbachev began engaging in talks to help repair relations between the two superpowers. But the steady decline of the Soviet Union's political structure and its ultimate fall were largely precipitated by internal fracturing as well as Gorbachev's moves to reform Communism in the region.

Soviet Republics and Satellite Countries

To understand the gradual breakdown of the Soviet Union, it helps to know the republics that made up the Soviet Union. From 1940 to 1991, the Soviet Union was made up of fifteen constituent republics: Armenia, Azerbaijan, Belorussia (now Belarus), Estonia, Georgia, Kazakhstan, Kirghizia (now Kyrgyzstan), Latvia, Lithuania, Moldavia (now Moldova), Russia, Tadzhikistan (now Tajikistan), Turkmenistan, Ukraine, and Uzbekistan.

Most of these republics were grouped into collective areas. For example, Estonia, Latvia, and Lithuania made up a region known as the Baltic states, as they were clustered around the eastern coast of the Baltic Sea. Armenia, Azerbaijan, and Georgia made up the Caucasus, as they lay near the Caucasus Mountains. (Technically, Iran, Russia,

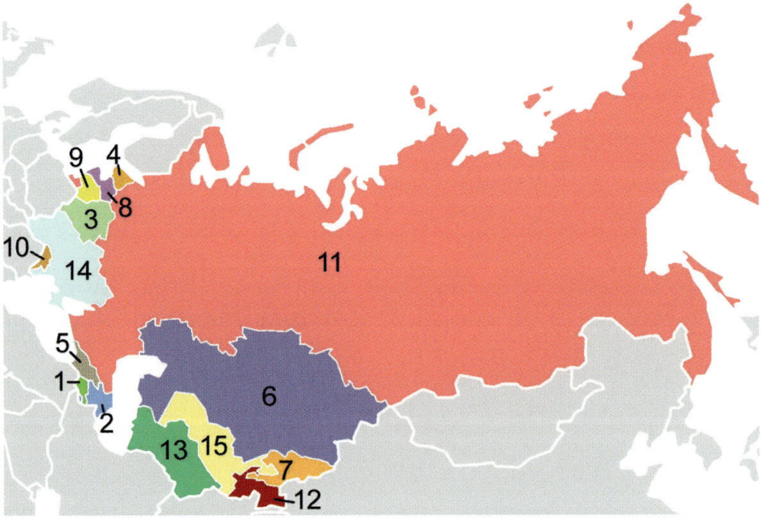

There were fifteen Soviet republics, and Russia was by far the largest.

and Turkey are also considered part of that region, though for the purpose of discussing the breakdown of the Soviet Union, Armenia, Azerbaijan, and Georgia were referred to as the Caucasus states.) Moldova, Ukraine, and Belarus were known as the Western republics. And Kazakhstan, Uzbekistan, Tajikistan, Turkmenistan, and Kyrgyzstan made up the central Asian republics.

In addition, the Soviet Union effectively controlled six satellite countries under the Warsaw Pact: Poland, East Germany, Czechoslovakia (now the Czech Republic), Hungary, Romania, and Bulgaria. (The Soviet Union had also controlled Yugoslavia and Albania for a time, though both of those ended their alignment with the Soviet Union long before the actual dissolution of the Soviet Union.) These satellite countries were independent in name but were effectively controlled by the Soviet Union.

For decades, all of these satellite countries had operated under the political structure of the Soviet Union. Although there were many branches to the government structure in the region, ultimately it was controlled by the **Politburo**, the highest-ranking level of government under the Communist Party of the Soviet Union. The Politburo was in charge of all Soviet policymaking. The Politburo and other branches of the Soviet government had long been filled by older, conservative members who weren't particularly interested in reform until Mikhail Gorbachev was elected general secretary of the Communist Party of the Soviet Union on March 11, 1985, which effectively placed him as the leader of the Soviet Union.

The Warsaw Pact

In this map of Europe and the Soviet Union circa 1973, the countries participating in the Warsaw Pact are displayed in red; the countries participating in NATO are in blue. The numbers represent each country's active military personnel.

Commonly called the Warsaw Pact, this defense treaty was officially named the Treaty of Friendship, Cooperation, and Mutual Assistance. But it's safe to say that "Warsaw Pact" rolled off the tongue better! It was established on May 14, 1955, and was essentially a collective security pact, like NATO. NATO was formed so that if one member nation were attacked, the other member nations would provide support. The Warsaw Pact had the same general goal. The Soviet Union and seven other European countries pledged to support each other if any member was attacked. During the Cold War, the members of NATO were essentially at war with the members of the Warsaw Pact, but there was never any direct conflict between them in Europe.

The eight members of the Warsaw Pact included the Soviet Union, Albania, Bulgaria, Czechoslovakia (now the Czech Republic), East Germany (known as the German Democratic Republic), Hungary, Poland, and Romania. When the Soviet Union began its final collapse in 1991, the Warsaw Pact disbanded as well. In the decades following, Warsaw Pact nations Poland, Hungary, the Czech Republic, Slovakia (formerly part of Czechoslovakia), Bulgaria, Romania, and Albania, as well as the Baltic states, joined NATO.

Communist Reform and a New Leader

When Gorbachev took office in 1985, he was fifty-four years old—young by Soviet leader standards. In fact, he was the first Soviet leader born after the Russian Revolution. He also had an eye on reform. He aimed to reform and modernize the Communist structure of the Soviet Union. Ultimately, his actions led to an end to the Communist superpower,

Mikhail Gorbachev wanted to modernize Communism in the Soviet Union, but under his rule, the Union eventually fell.

but that wasn't his original intent. He simply wanted to modernize an aging political system to help revitalize the Soviet economy.

The Soviet economy was struggling, and Gorbachev felt the road to economic revitalization could be traveled by enacting both political and social reform. Perestroika and glasnost were two ways Gorbachev worked toward this reform.

Perestroika: Restructuring

Perestroika literally means "rebuilding" or "restructuring." Gorbachev introduced perestroika as a means to strengthen the Soviet Union's economy. He was in favor of the socialist system in the Soviet Union but felt that it didn't work efficiently enough for the Soviet population. The standard of living for people in the Soviet Union was poor, and economic development had slowed.

At the time, the Soviet Union was effectively a **command economy**. In such an economy, the government controls pricing, distribution, and production, and industries are publicly owned. This is directly counter to the United States' market economy, in which pricing, distribution, and production are based on supply and demand and industries can be privately or publicly owned. Gorbachev's perestroika didn't seek to destroy the command economy of the Soviet Union, but it did introduce some elements of a market economy.

For example, the Law on State Enterprises, enacted in 1987, allowed state-run industries to adopt a supply-and-demand strategy when determining production.

The industries were still publicly owned with decisions made collectively, rather than by a private owner, but the decisions were now based on supply and demand, as would be the case in a market economy. And the decision makers were no longer government ministries; the law shifted the decision-making power to elected workers' collectives. The law also shifted financial accountability to the enterprises. While the government used to assist enterprises that weren't profitable, under the new law enterprises had to cover employee wages, taxes, and supplies through their revenue. This, too, is more similar to a market economy than a command economy.

In 1988, Gorbachev's economic reform took another step toward a market economy when the Law of Cooperatives was enacted. This law allowed for private ownership of service and manufacturing businesses, as well as in the foreign-trade sector, which had previously been solely controlled by the Ministry of Foreign Trade. However, it still was not a true market economy because the law also enacted restrictions on employment and high taxes that were a deterrent to those who might consider private ownership of a business. People could own a business, but they had to be able to afford the taxes, and they had to abide by the employment restrictions. These restrictions and high taxes were eventually eased, but initially they were quite a deterrent to private ownership of business.

In addition to relaxing restrictions on foreign trade, Gorbachev's perestroika allowed foreign investors to form joint ventures with Soviet enterprises and cooperatives. This meant that foreign entities could form a partnership with a Soviet entity in which the Soviet entity provided labor, infrastructure, and a market, and the foreign entity provided capital, technology, expertise, and sometimes needed products and services. Such ventures weren't uncommon in market economies, but they had been unheard of in the Soviet Union's command economy.

Although Gorbachev's reforms were considered radical by many and were intended to revitalize the Soviet economy, in reality they were probably too little, too late, and they actually ended up further breaking down the economy. The hybrid system of command and market economies resulted in a fall in **gross domestic product**, a decline in government tax revenues with an increase in government spending, and an overall instability of the government's control over the economy.

Glasnost: Freedom of the Press

Perestroika was a means to achieve economic reform while glasnost was meant to work on social reform. Glasnost technically means "publicity," but more specifically it refers to an openness to publicity and public information. In the United States, it would be similar to freedom of speech and freedom of the press. In the Soviet Union, it meant more transparency in the Soviet government's activities and institutions.

Prior to Gorbachev being elected leader of the Soviet Union, Soviet media was controlled by the government. **Censorship** was heavy—anything broadcast or printed had to be approved by the government. All production facilities for television, radio, and newspaper, magazine, and book production were state-owned, and thus the Soviets could

Americans march for peace at Red Square in Moscow, circa 1961.

easily control what was produced. Because they couldn't control what was broadcast by foreign radio stations, they simply jammed the foreign radio signals.

By censoring all forms of information sharing, the government was able to control what citizens knew of government activities and, by extension, squash any ideas of revolution or independence. If Soviet citizens didn't know of political unrest in the Soviet republics or satellite countries, in theory they wouldn't be inspired to take any sort of political action on their own.

This censorship essentially allowed the Soviet Union to write its own history. They simply destroyed anything that contradicted the history they wanted recorded for posterity. Anyone caught reading or listening to anything not approved by the government was subject to prosecution.

Censorship in the Soviet Union was at its worst under Joseph Stalin's rule, but it also existed while Nikita Khrushchev was in power (1955–1964), albeit slightly relaxed. It continued through the reigns of leaders Leonid Brezhnev (1964–1982), Yuri Andropov (1982–1984), and Konstantin Chernenko (1984–1985). Soviet censorship, while relaxed compared to Stalin's standards, was considered to be among the tightest in the world.

When Gorbachev came into power, he aimed to substantially decrease censorship as a means of making the government more transparent to citizens. Previously, the government had complete control over all aspects of the economy as well as all aspects of managing the Soviet Union. This resulted in corruption and abuse of administrative power by high-ranking Soviet officials. Gorbachev felt that allowing more transparency in the government and giving citizens more say in the workings of the government would ultimately promote a healthier economic and political structure.

Soviet citizens barely knew what to make of glasnost when it began. They were dubious of government claims that they could now speak about things previously forbidden. Slowly, they began to exercise their right to free speech and their right to be heard. And just as perestroika took a turn that Gorbachev had not anticipated, so did glasnost. As citizens gained more access to public information when uncensored radio broadcasts were permitted and the broadcasting of CNN became allowed (in 1989), they also gained more confidence in expressing their views. Ultimately, their newfound access to information and ability to express their views led many to become disillusioned with the government. Citizens learned of problems that the Soviet government had long covered up, including pollution, high mortality rates, food shortages, unacceptable housing conditions, and state crimes against citizens. They also learned about Western culture and the quality of life in Western Europe and the United States, and it was in stark contrast to the quality of life they experienced in the Soviet Union.

Perhaps most damaging to the Soviet Union, citizens became aware of the weaknesses in the Communist system under which they had been living for decades. When they saw those weaknesses and the possibilities that could be available under another political structure, it was yet another major chip at the foundation underlying the Soviet Union.

Uprisings

In addition to perestroika and glasnost, a further major contributor to the fall of the Soviet Union was a number of **nationalist** uprisings that took place in the individual Soviet republics. Most of the early ones occurred in small republics. (Russia was by far the largest republic in the Soviet Union,

A 1989 protest in the Estonian capital city of Tallinn

and it remained relatively stable for quite a while.) But even those small fractures were enough to destabilize the power of the Soviet Union as a whole.

Unrest in the Baltic States

The unrest in the Baltic republics came early—perhaps not surprising, since they had been forcibly made part of the Soviet Union under the Molotov-Ribbentrop Pact in 1939, which was an agreement between Hitler and Soviet leader Joseph Stalin. Thousands of citizens in Latvia and Estonia held protests in 1987 commemorating the Molotov Pact, the Latvian deportation in 1941 (a product of Stalin), the Estonian War of Independence (1918–1920), and the establishment of phosphate mines in Estonia. The Soviet Union under Gorbachev's rule did not stop these protests, whereas they certainly would've been ceased under earlier governments. Citizens were gaining confidence in their ability to express their political, economic, and social ideas.

In 1988, Estonia passed laws that allowed it, as a republic, to reject Soviet laws that challenged their local autonomy. Essentially, these laws represented a resistance against the central Soviet government controlling Estonia. They established the political organization called the Estonian Popular Front, and their previously conservative Communist leader was replaced by the more liberal Vaino Väljas, who ultimately allowed the Estonian Popular Front to reestablish the Estonian flag as the national flag of Estonia and to make Estonian the official language of the republic. In short, the Estonian Popular Front and Väljas allowed much more autonomy in Estonia than had been allowed for decades.

National unrest was brewing in Latvia as well, where an anti-Soviet, anti-Communist human rights group known as Helsinki-86 had formed and was openly protesting Soviet rule. In 1988, just as Estonia had done, Latvia established the Latvian Popular Front, and their former Communist leader, Boris Pugo, was replaced by a more liberal leader, Jänis Vagris. Like Estonia had done, the Latvian Popular Front and Vagris agreed to make the Latvian flag the republic's official flag and Latvian the country's official language.

The same held true in Lithuania—an older conservative leader was replaced by a more liberal one (Algirdas Mykolas

Brazauskas). In addition, the Lithuanian flag was reinstated as the national flag, and Lithuanian became the republic's official language. Lithuania's move toward independence was further strengthened when, in 1989, thirty-six of the forty-two Lithuanian delegates to the Congress of People's Deputies (at the time, the newly formed and highest body of state authority in the Soviet Union) were not from the Communist Party of Lithuania, but instead from Sajūdis, the nationalist movement in the republic. By the end of 1989, even the Communist Party of Lithuania was resisting Soviet control. They split from the Communist Party of the Soviet Union (CPSU), and Lithuania was declared formally independent from Soviet control.

It's worth noting that the replacement of conservative leaders in all three Baltic republics was done by Gorbachev, who believed that more liberal leadership would help the Soviet Union as a whole build a more modern, workable, political and economic structure. Gorbachev also publicly supported the condemnation of the Molotov-Ribbentrop Pact that had led to Soviet control of the region in the first place—another important step toward independence in the Baltic republics and another crack in the Soviet structure.

In 1990, Gorbachev recommended to the CPSU that the party allow the Soviet republics to hold competitive elections in which Communist leaders and nationalist leaders could be up for election. The CPSU agreed to the recommendation, and the ultimate result was that the CPSU lost its hold in six republics, including the three Baltic republics. Lithuania became the first republic to officially break from the Soviet Union on March 11, 1990. Estonia followed suit weeks later, and Latvia declared independence on May 4, 1990.

Unrest in the Caucasus

Protests began in the Caucasus in 1987 as well. Some had to do with environmental concerns—a chemical plant, a nuclear plant, air pollution, and the condition of Lake Sevan. But other protests had to do with an ongoing struggle for Armenian national rights. Armenia and Azerbaijan were both Soviet republics that had interest in the disputed territories of Nagorno-Karabakh and Nakhchivan. There was considerable ethnic tension between the Azeris and the Armenians as well, which resulted in numerous protests, demonstrations, and sometimes violence. Eventually, these tensions resulted in the Armenia-Azerbaijan War (1988–1994), which further destabilized the Soviet's political control in the region. Levon Ter-Petrossian, the chairman of Armenia's Pan-Armenian National Movement and later president of Armenia, began considering a movement toward Armenian independence from the Soviet Union.

But even before the war, the Armenian uprising was strong. Both Armenia and Azerbaijan protested and fought over their ethnic differences and their disputed territories, but in the late 1980s, Armenia took bold steps that the Azeris had not yet taken. When Gorbachev replaced Armenia's leader with Suren Harutyunyan, Harutyunyan wasted no time in making changes. Within a week of his appointment, he had replaced the Soviet flag with the Armenian flag as the republic's national flag. And within three weeks of his appointment, he had formally approved the plan to make Nagorno-Karabakh (one of the disputed territories) part of Armenia.

During the competitive elections in 1990, Armenia voted out the Communist Party in favor of the Petrossian-led Pan-Armenian National Movement. Azerbaijan's elections, which took place later in 1990, were full of corruption, intimidation, and even murder, and the ultimate result was that Azerbaijan remained a Soviet republic at that time.

Although overshadowed by the events in Armenia and Azerbaijan at the same time, Georgia was quietly beginning to protest, too, calling for Georgian independence from the Soviet Union. In 1989, after Soviet troops attacked Georgian protestors, resulting in twenty deaths and more than two hundred wounded, that desire for independence was solidified among many Georgians. Like Armenia, in 1990, Georgia voted out the Soviet Communist Party and instead elected the Round Table-Free Georgia.

Unrest in the Western Republics

By 1988, the Western republics were beginning to join the fray too. Moldovans held organizations and protests calling for Romanian to be reinstituted as the republic's official language. They also wanted to return to Moldovan traditions, which had long been suppressed by Soviet traditions. Moldova took a major step toward independence in 1990, when it elected the Popular Front of Moldova over the Soviet Communist Party.

In Ukraine, citizens demonstrated on the second anniversary of the Chernobyl disaster that took place on April 26, 1986. Shortly thereafter, thousands gathered in the city of Lviv to protest the list of delegates to the nineteenth

Communist Party—delegates in which the public had no confidence. Further demonstrations, protests, and gatherings supported independence, human rights, and Ukrainian Catholicism, which had long been suppressed under Soviet rule. Ukraine—in particular, the cities of Lviv and Kiev—was the site of many protests in 1989 as they grew bolder in their rights to religious freedom. By late 1989, Ukrainian had once again been declared the republic's official language, and a major Russian Orthodox Church in Lviv had established itself as a Ukrainian Greek Catholic Church. Ukrainian Catholics could, in theory, worship without persecution for the first time in a very long time. However, Ukrainian independence was a long and difficult battle. After many months of political maneuvering, protests, and resignations, the Party of Democratic Rebirth of Ukraine was finally founded in December, 1990.

In Belarus, the Belarusian Popular Front (BPF) formed as a political party supporting independence for the republic. In 1989, thousands of citizens of Belarus protested their local leaders and demanded additional cleanup of the contaminated Chernobyl site.

Unrest in the Central Asian Republics

In 1986, the Jeltoqsan riots were the first obvious signs of unrest among the central Asian republics. The riots took place in Kazakhstan, when Gorbachev installed Gennady Kolbin, a Russian, as the first secretary of the Communist Party of Kazakhstan. The seat had previously been held by Dinmukhamed Kunayev, a native Kazakh who was generally liked in part because under his rule, many Kazakhs held high positions in the government and economic and educational institutions. Gorbachev dismissed Kunayev on the grounds of corruption, but Kazakh citizens were displeased that a Russian who had never lived in Kazakhstan was being placed as their high government official. Upset citizens protested, and the situation escalated into a riot that took several days to control and resulted in deaths and imprisonments. Just a few years later, in 1989, Gorbachev removed Kolbin after he mishandled riots that broke out in Kazakhstan in June 1989, and replaced him with another ethnic Kazhak, Nursultan Nazarbayev, who ultimately led Kazhakstan to independence.

In Uzbekistan in 1989, as he had done in numerous other Soviet republics, Gorbachev replaced the first secretary of the republic's Communist Party with a more liberal choice, Islam Karimov, who ultimately led Uzbekistan to become an independent state.

In early 1990, Tajikistan was the site of anti-government riots involving Armenian refugees and nationalist Tajiks. Protestors burned and looted government buildings and stores, hundreds of people were injured, and twenty-six people died.

Unrest in Russia

One major factor in the collapse of the Soviet Union was the tension between Soviet leader Gorbachev and Russian Boris Yeltsin. Yeltsin had worked as part of Gorbachev's government. Gorbachev had appointed him to the CPSU Central Committee Secretariat, a branch of the government responsible for central administration of the Communist

Party—that is, while the Politburo drafted policies and laws, CPSU administered them. But in late 1987, Yeltsin abruptly resigned and detailed his reasons why in a letter to Gorbachev—among them, the slow pace of reform under perestroika. When Gorbachev didn't respond by addressing Yeltsin's complaints, Yeltsin criticized the leader in front of the Central Committee of the Communist Party, an action that was pretty much unheard of in the Soviet Union at that time. Word of Yeltsin's dissent quietly spread, and Yeltsin became a sort of rebel hero for the anti–Soviet Union groups.

In 1990, Yeltsin was elected to the Congress of People's Deputies of Russia, and that same year he was elected chair of the Presidium of the Supreme Soviet (a leading position) of the Russian Soviet Federative Socialist Republic (RSFSR). Shortly thereafter, the RSFSR declared itself **sovereign** from the Soviet Union, and by July 1990, Yeltsin had officially resigned from the Communist Party. In 1991, over Gorbachev's objections, Yeltsin won the seat of president of the RSFSR.

Loss of Satellite Countries

Although technically the satellite countries were independent, they were essentially under Soviet rule. However, Gorbachev opposed the Brezhnev Doctrine, which was the policy that held them under Soviet control. He abandoned it, and in 1989, the Communist government fell in Warsaw after the country experimented with democracy. This event led the five other Warsaw Pact satellite countries to similarly overthrow their Communist rule by the end of 1989.

The 1991 Soviet Coup

Although many Soviet republics declared independence from the Soviet Union in 1990, the conflict didn't end there. Soviet troops tried to suppress independence in the Baltic states. But in many regions, every attempt the Soviet Union made to attempt to regain centralized control was met with further resolve for independence. Gorbachev decided to restructure the Soviet Union into a federation of independent states with a common president, military, and foreign policy—in a way, similar to the structure of the United States. His plan was known as the New Union Treaty.

Some of the republics, such as those in central Asia, supported Gorbachev's plan, as they didn't feel their economies were strong enough to exist independently. They were willing to accept that the Communist Party would

Gennady Yanayev led the group that attempted to unseat Gorbachev during the 1991 coup.

A Long-Awaited Obituary

The day after Christmas in 1991, Americans got the news they had been waiting decades for—the superpower Soviet Union, a constant looming threat in the Cold War, was no more. The *New York Times* headline read: "END OF THE SOVIET UNION: The Soviet State, Born of a Dream, Dies."

Although it was written about a group of countries, the article was written with tongue-in-cheek, in the style of an obituary:

> The Soviet state, marked throughout its brief but tumultuous history by great achievement and terrible suffering, died today after a long and painful decline. It was 74 years old. Conceived in utopian promise and born in the violent upheavals of the "Great October Revolution of 1917," the union heaved its last in the dreary darkness of late December 1991, stripped of ideology, dismembered, bankrupt and hungry—but awe-inspiring even in its fall.

The article, at times factual but at times clever and poetic, went on to say, "Measured against its own ambitions, the USSR died a monumental failure. … In the end, promising a new life, it created an unspeakably bleak society—polluted, chronically short of everything, stripped of initiative and spirituality. While the bulk of the nation stood in line or guzzled rot-gut vodka, the Communist elite raised corruption to new heights."

The article's irreverent style is perhaps fitting, though. Gorbachev's glasnost embraced a free press that made the government more transparent, and this was certainly an example of a newspaper stripping aside all pretense and showing the Soviet government in its ugly, unvarnished truth.

still exercise some control over their republics if it meant they could reap the benefits of a common economic market. However, those interested in a more comprehensive reform, such as Boris Yeltsin, opposed the plan and felt that the best option was for states to become independent. Conservatives who supported the Soviet Union strongly opposed the New Union Treaty, as they felt it weakened the power structure of the Soviet Union.

Gorbachev's vice president, Gennady Yanayev, was one who opposed the treaty. Along with Prime Minister Valentin Pavlov, Defense Minister Dmitry Yzov, KGB chief Vladimir Kryuchkov, and several other senior government officials, Yanayev led a **coup d'état** attempt on August 19, 1991, which put Gorbachev on house arrest so he could not sign the treaty. Among the many people who opposed the coup was Boris Yeltsin, who publicly decried it and gained much support in doing so. The coup lasted only three days, due in large part to a lack of popular support. It seemed the public wasn't as interested in retaining the structure of the Soviet Union as the higher-ups had hoped.

Gorbachev returned to power after the coup, but his support was shaky. It was the beginning of the end for the Soviet Union. Within days, Gorbachev had essentially dissolved the CPSU and ended Communist rule. In the four months that followed, ten republics declared their independence, and Yeltsin began to take over the pieces of the Soviet government that remained. On December 25, 1991, Gorbachev officially resigned as president of the Soviet Union and transferred all powers to Yeltsin. The Soviet Union was officially no more.

Joseph Stalin and Nikita Khrushchev, circa 1936, are shown here together when the two were still collaborating.

CHAPTER THREE

The Faces of the Cold War

The Cold War was a long, protracted conflict between the world's two superpowers—the United States and the Soviet Union. The actual fall of the Soviet Union was a relatively short period during the Cold War. It can be loosely defined as beginning in 1985, when Gorbachev took office and began implementing his reform efforts, and ending with Gorbachev's resignation and the official fall of the Soviet Union at the end of 1991. However, there were certainly factors before Gorbachev took office that began to chip away at the foundations of the Soviet Union—namely, the arms race and space race with the United States that weakened the Soviet Union's economy.

When Gorbachev took office, he walked into a nation in an economic slump, in part because of the money past administrations had spent on developing arms and other technologies. So while Gorbachev's attempts at political and social reform, designed to stimulate economic prosperity, were direct causes of the Soviet Union's fall, it would be remiss not to consider the decisions of leaders before him when looking at the decline of the superpower.

Joseph Stalin

As the leader of the Soviet Union when the United States dropped the atomic bombs on Hiroshima and Nagasaki, Joseph Stalin reacted swiftly and ordered that the Soviet Union must devote large amounts of money and resources to developing atomic weaponry that could compctc with that of the United States. His allotment of money to developing arms, rather than using funds to rebuild the war-ravaged nation, was a significant factor in the crumbled economy that Gorbachev inherited when he took office decades later.

Stalin: The Early Years

Joseph Stalin was born Ioseb Dzhugashvili (Stalin was a pseudonym he adopted in the early 1900s) in Georgia on December 18, 1878, to a cobbler father and a housemaid mother. His father was not a steady presence in the family. An abusive alcoholic, he left the family after he was banished from their town for assaulting the police chief.

Stalin's childhood was one of ill health and misfortune. He was born with two toes adjoined, he suffered smallpox at age seven and ended up with facial scarring as a result, and he suffered a permanent injury to his arm in a carriage accident when he was twelve. Stalin won a scholarship to the **seminary**, and he was a strong student who enjoyed politics, reading, and writing poetry, but he was expelled from the seminary in 1899.

Joseph Stalin proved to be a ruthless leader.

By this time, Stalin had discovered the work of Russian Communist Vladimir Lenin, and shortly after Stalin's expulsion from the seminary, he went underground as a revolutionary for the Marxist Russian Social-Democratic Labour Party, the precursor to the **Bolsheviks**.

Eventually, Lenin officially formed the Bolsheviks, and the bright, capable, charming Stalin joined him. Stalin, a gifted writer, assisted in the creation and dissemination of propaganda and helped organize strikes. However, the funding for these activities often came from illegal—and sometimes deadly—means, so Stalin was arrested and exiled multiple times. Stalin was as gifted at escaping exile as he was at writing, so his exiles rarely lasted long.

Stalin's Rise to Power

Stalin's mentor, Lenin, eventually became the head of the Russian Soviet Federative Socialist Republic (RSFSR) and later the Soviet Union, and it was Lenin who appointed Stalin as general secretary of the Communist Party of the Soviet Union in 1922—the same post that Gorbachev would hold decades later. Although Stalin and Lenin began as allies, as Stalin grew in power, Lenin began to disagree with him, and their relationship began to falter, with Lenin eventually declaring that Stalin should be removed as general secretary. By then, though, Lenin was in poor health, and the situation was out of his control.

When Lenin died in 1924, Stalin was one of a number of powerful men in the Politburo. In the following years, Stalin systematically removed all of his internal enemies and opponents—some were fired, some were imprisoned, and some were executed. As head of the Soviet Union, Stalin was well known for using the secret police and intelligence agencies to carry out his own agenda (such as assassinating Leon Trotsky, fellow member of the Politburo with whom Stalin had numerous political disagreements) and to maintain a strong Communist Party and tight control over the media and over Soviet citizens.

Stalin was also known for his extremely healthy ego. He elevated himself to almost godlike status, even going so far as to essentially rewrite history to reflect a strongly pro-Stalin Soviet history. He was militant about censoring the media so that Soviet citizens only had access to pro–Soviet Union and pro-Stalin news and information. Anyone who dared speak against Stalin, Communism, or the Soviet Union would be exiled, sentenced to a **gulag**, or executed.

Part of Stalin's rewriting of Soviet history was designed to cover up some of his most heinous acts, such as the ethnic purges he conducted. In the late 1930s, hundreds of thousands of non-native people in the Soviet Union were arrested, with many of them executed. These ethnicities included Polish, German, Korean, and American people in the Soviet Union, among other ethnicities. Most of these people were ordinary citizens—they were not officials in the Soviet government who would have been a political threat to Stalin. They simply didn't fit Stalin's view of the populace of the Soviet Union. Of the people, Stalin reportedly said, "Who's going to remember all this riff-raff in ten or twenty years' time? No one." Clearly, he thought the same of the 3.3 million people that he ordered deported to Siberia and other central Asian republics in the 1940s, nearly half of whom ended up dying of disease or malnutrition.

Stalin's Contribution to the Fall of the Soviet Union

Part of Stalin's strategy for running the Soviet Union as a Communist nation involved the collectivization of agriculture, in which farmers are part of cooperative organizations, rather than family-run enterprises. Stalin insisted this would improve the standard of living for peasant farmers, but in reality the opposite was true. Stalin's collectivized agricultural system instead resulted in decreased output, widespread famine and death, and mass murder and deportation as Stalin worked to implement his plan.

Stalin had similar ideas about industrialization. He believed in a state-controlled industrialization plan, and he ruthlessly enforced it. This did result in short-term economic prosperity for the Soviet Union where industrialization was concerned, but at the expense of millions of deaths. This economic growth did enable the Soviet Union to remain strong during World War II; however, it's thought that a total of about three million Soviet citizens died during Stalin's reign, so one has to weigh that when considering whether the economic growth under Stalin strengthened the Soviet Union or ultimately weakened it. A mass loss of citizens—and the resulting loss of trust from other citizens—is not a recipe for a strong nation.

Nor was Stalin's prioritization of weapons technology over human aid after World War II. Although the Soviet Union did not fall to the Nazis during World War II, the nation was certainly devastated by fighting—roughly twenty-six million Soviet citizens were killed in the war, and twenty-five million had been left homeless. Several major cities lay in rubble, too. Clearly, economic resources were needed to rebuild the devastated Soviet Union. Instead, Stalin declared that development of nuclear weapons was the nation's top priority, after seeing the devastation the United States' nuclear weapons had wrought on Hiroshima and Nagasaki in Japan. Stalin knew the Soviet Union needed to keep up with the United States in terms of weaponry.

Ultimately, the Soviet Union collapsed in part due to a growing lack of citizen support. The disillusionment with the Soviet Union grew when censorship was eased during Gorbachev's time in office, and Soviet citizens began to learn more about Soviet history—the truth, not the Stalin-rewritten version. When people saw the lack of support for common citizens over the decades, such as when Stalin prioritized technology over people's welfare or when he prioritized his industrial and agriculture goals over human welfare, they began to rebel against the Communist government, and the Soviet Union began to falter. But the seeds for that unrest were planted by Stalin during his time as leader of the Soviet Union.

Nikita Khrushchev

When Stalin died in March 1953, Georgy Malenkov took over as the leader of the Soviet Union. However, he was replaced after two years by Nikita Khrushchev, who held the position from 1953 to 1964 and played an important role in the arms race and the space race that contributed to the deterioration of the Soviet Union.

Nikita Khrushchev originally supported Stalin, but the two eventually broke apart.

Khrushchev: The Early Years

Khrushchev was born on April 15, 1894, in a poverty-stricken Russian village near the present-day border with Ukraine. He was born to peasant parents and attended school very minimally. As a teen, he moved with his father (and later his mother and sister) to a more industrialized city and found a position as a metal fitter's apprentice, which led to his later employment as a metal worker. Khrushchev's father, Sergei, was a union organizer, and Khrushchev shared his beliefs as a teen, becoming involved in various strikes and protests.

Like Stalin, Khrushchev eventually joined the Bolsheviks. He held a number of smaller, local political positions before being elected to the Fourteenth Congress of the USSR Communist Party in 1925. Khrushchev was a disciple of Lazar Kaganovich, a close associate of Stalin, and he was also acquainted with Nadezhda Alliluyeva, Stalin's second wife, from their time together at the Stalin Industrial Academy. These two associations helped Khrushchev move up in the ranks in Stalin's government, despite his peasant background and lack of schooling.

Khrushchev's Rise to Power

By 1932, Khrushchev was attending meetings with Stalin, and the two had formed a close relationship. Khrushchev openly supported Stalin's executions and deportments during the **Great Purge** even though years later, he denounced them. And while serving as first secretary of the Moscow Regional Committee of the CPSU, Khrushchev turned a blind eye when thirty-five of the top thirty-eight party officials—his colleagues and many of them his friends—were executed under Stalin's regime.

As a party leader, Khrushchev was responsible for ordering the arrest or execution of so-called enemies to Stalin's government to fulfill a quota set by the Politburo. In the summer of 1937, after receiving the order to help fulfill the quota, Khrushchev reported that he had ordered the arrest of 41,305 "enemies" and recommended execution for 8,500 of them.

In short, Khrushchev did anything and everything required to support Stalin's government. He was rewarded when Stalin appointed him the head of the Communist Party in Ukraine. However, when the Nazis invaded the Soviet Union in the early 1940s, Khrushchev's unwavering support of Stalin began to falter. He felt Stalin made questionable military decisions that resulted in mass casualties and unnecessary loss in the **Red Army**.

In the post-war years, when Stalin was enforcing his agricultural collectivism plan, resulting in famine that was particularly devastating in Ukraine, Khrushchev's relationship with Stalin further deteriorated. They quarreled over the republic's need for aid, and eventually Khrushchev lost his position as party leader in Ukraine when Stalin sent Khrushchev's former mentor, Kaganovich, in to help him. Khrushchev was later reinstated as party leader in Ukraine and regained a position in Stalin's trusted circle. Khrushchev was present at Stalin's bedside after he died and reportedly wept.

At some point, though, Khrushchev's devotion to Stalin shifted. In his memoirs, Khrushchev reflected on Stalin's policy of deporting or executing those he saw as enemies to the party (a process Khrushchev had once willingly participated in): "Everyone lived in fear in those days. … People not to Stalin's liking were annihilated, honest party members, irreproachable people, loyal and hard workers for our cause. … This was utter and complete arbitrariness. And now is all this to be forgiven and forgotten? Never!"

After Stalin's death, the leadership of the Soviet Union could have been assumed by several high-ranking members of the Communist Party. Ultimately, leadership went to Khrushchev, after two years of political maneuverings.

Khrushchev's Contribution to the Fall of the Soviet Union

As leader of the Soviet Union, Khrushchev relaxed (slightly) some of the censorship that Stalin had put in place. When Gorbachev followed suit and further relaxed censorship, it was a major factor in weakening the Communist rule of the Soviet Union. Stalin had whitewashed the negative and gory parts of the history under his rule, and relaxed censorship meant that people became increasingly aware of the atrocities done to citizens. There was still heavy censorship under Khrushchev, but not as heavy as under Stalin, and thus it presented a very slight crack in the Soviet Union's armor.

More damaging to the fabric of the Soviet Union was Khrushchev's desire to keep up with the United States in arms and space technology. Stalin had set the stage with his desire to keep up with or exceed the United States in weapons technology, with cost being no object, and Khrushchev followed suit. Khrushchev was known for his bold, boastful statements (some true, some hyperbole), and during the Cold War, he bragged about the Soviets' superiority where missiles were concerned, even going so far as to challenge the United States to a missile shooting match to see which nation had the superior arms.

Throughout the late 1940s and the 1950s, the United States and the Soviet Union were locked in a constant battle to see which superpower had superior weapons technology. The Soviet Union developed an atomic bomb (detonated in

A Former Disciple Turns on His Mentor

Khrushchev was initially a strong supporter of Stalin, but at some point, his views about the tyrannical leader shifted—at least publicly. In a speech given to the Twentieth Congress of the CPSU in February 1956, Khrushchev denounced Stalin in no uncertain terms. In particular, he addressed the **cult of personality** that had grown around Stalin:

> It is impermissible and foreign to the spirit of Marxism-Leninism to elevate one person, to transform him into a superman possessing supernatural characteristics, akin to those of a god. ... Such a belief about a man, and

Stalin painted himself as a hero, and the public bought into the image—for a time.

> specifically about Stalin, was cultivated among us for many years. … At present, we are concerned with a question which has immense importance for the Party now and for the future—with how the cult of the person of Stalin has been gradually growing, the cult which became at a certain specific stage the source of a whole series of exceedingly serious and grave perversions of Party principles, of Party democracy, of revolutionary legality.

Khrushchev went on to present letters from other government officials who had been subject to Stalin's uncontrolled ego and stated that Stalin's "negative characteristics … developed steadily and during the last years acquired an absolutely insufferable character." In the interest of keeping history from repeating itself, Khrushchev spared no words in describing Stalin as a leader who "practiced brutal violence, not only toward everything which opposed him, but also toward that which seemed, to his capricious and despotic character, contrary to his concepts. … Whoever opposed these concepts or tried to prove his [own] viewpoint and the correctness of his [own] position was doomed to removal from the leadership collective and to subsequent moral and physical annihilation." The speech left no doubt that Khrushchev wanted to paint Stalin as a tyrant—a fact that most people would not argue, but that was somewhat surprising coming from a man who had recently wept at Stalin's deathbed.

1949, just four years after the United States dropped atomic bombs on Japan), and in the early 1950s, both superpowers raced to develop hydrogen bombs. The Soviets gained the upper hand in the race in 1957, when they launched both the first **intercontinental ballistic missile** (ICBM) and *Sputnik*. These developments proved that the Soviets could basically send a nuclear weapon to strike anywhere in the world and gave them the lead in the space race.

This technology development came at a hefty price, though. Billions (perhaps trillions, but exact totals are nearly impossible to determine) were spent on arms and space technology in both the United States and the Soviet Union during the Cold War, but the struggling Soviet economy could not withstand such a financial hit. They were still trying to rebuild after World War II. However, the food shortages, famine, and other devastation during Stalin's regime as well as all the money spent on weapons and space technology meant that little rebuilding could be done. This had a negative impact on the stability of the Soviet Union. Citizens were tired of living in poor housing conditions and without enough food. They began to doubt their government's structure, as many people's lives were difficult and showing no signs of improvement.

When Khrushchev was removed from power in 1964, the Soviet economy was weak and the social structure was further cracking. Several successive leaders, including Leonid Brezhnev, Yuri Andropov, and Konstantin Chernenko, did little to repair the faltering Soviet Union, and by the time Gorbachev took control in 1985, the Soviet economy was quite weak, and he felt extensive reform was the only way to strengthen the superpower's political structure.

Mikhail Gorbachev

While Stalin's reign of terror, corruption, and censorship created a Soviet Union that was bound to fracture, and both Stalin's and Khrushchev's excessive spending on weapons and technology contributed to a fragile economy, Mikhail Gorbachev was probably the most prominent figure contributing to the collapse of the Soviet Union. Whether his reforms were a matter of too little too late or simply a system destined to fail remains debatable, but it's clear that Gorbachev's attempts at reform backfired badly and resulted in the cracked foundation of the Soviet Union.

Gorbachev: The Early Years

Mikhail Gorbachev was born on March 2, 1931, in the Russian village of Privolnoye. His family was of mixed Russian and Ukrainian heritage, and like Khrushchev's parents, Gorbachev's parents were peasant farmers. Both of Gorbachev's grandfathers were victims of Stalin's tyranny—both were arrested on false charges, and one was exiled to Siberia.

Unlike Khrushchev, Gorbachev was well educated. He worked on collective farms as a teen but also attended school, and in 1955, he earned his law degree from Moscow State University. He earned a master's degree in 1967 as well. It was during his university time that Gorbachev became a member of the Communist Party.

Gorbachev's ideas for reform showed promise, but in practice they led to the fall of the Soviet Union.

Gorbachev's Rise to Power

Gorbachev rose quickly through the ranks of the CPSU. After holding positions in local branches of the party, he was elected first party secretary of the Stavropol Regional Committee (a committee serving the Stavropol Krai region in Russia). At the age of thirty-nine, Gorbachev was one of the youngest provincial party chiefs in the Soviet Union. Stavropol Krai was a largely agricultural region, and Gorbachev helped improve farmers' living conditions, expand the size of their private farm plots, reorganize the collective farms in the region, and give farm workers a stronger voice in agricultural planning. Not surprisingly, this made him popular as a leader in the region.

Just a year later, he became part of the Communist Party Central Committee—the highest body of the CPSU. He moved up in the ranks there as well, and by 1979, he had been elected to the Politburo. While Yuri Andropov was leader of the Soviet Union, Gorbachev began working to replace older members of the party with younger members—a practice that Gorbachev continued when he became leader of the Soviet Union. Gorbachev had his eye on modernizing the Communist system in the Soviet Union, and he felt the older, more conservative party members would not be effective in achieving that vision. Newer, more liberal-minded party members were needed, in his view. And many party members agreed with Gorbachev—in fact, that was part of what eventually won Gorbachev the position of General Secretary of the CPSU. When Andropov died, despite his desire for Gorbachev to be the next head of the Soviet Union, elderly

Konstantin Chernenko took the seat. However, Chernenko died the next year, and the party recognized that a younger leader would be a more prudent choice. And so, at age fifty-four, Gorbachev was elected general secretary of the CPSU by the Politburo in 1985.

Gorbachev's Contribution to the Fall of the Soviet Union

There is no doubt that Gorbachev inherited a mess when he took over as the head of the Soviet Union. The nation's economy was unstable, and many citizens were disillusioned because their living conditions were bleak.

Gorbachev's answer to this mess was reform. He still believed strongly in a Communist nation, but he felt the Soviet Union's system needed an overhaul. Within a year of taking office, he had introduced his plans for perestroika and glasnost as well as *demokratizatsiya* (roughly defined as democratization). Although Gorbachev still supported a Communist government, he wanted to introduce some elements of democracy into it by allowing multiple candidates for the local CPSU elections. All candidates would still be from the Communist Party, to maintain the single-party system in the Soviet Union, but at least there would be some choice among the candidates.

Another of Gorbachev's reform initiatives was *uskoreniye*, which literally translates to acceleration. This initiative consisted of a plan to hasten the Soviet Union's social and economic development by overhauling heavy industry. Uskoreniye was a dismal failure because it required a mass infusion of capital into the heavy industries, which weakened the already struggling Soviet economy even more and destabilized the value of the Soviet dollar (the ruble).

Gorbachev introduced further reform by systematically replacing "old guard" party officials with younger, more liberal officials. He felt that reform demanded more liberal party members, but that strategy may have run away from him a bit. Some of the more liberal-minded officials who came into power under Gorbachev ended up being champions for regional independence, which was ultimately a major factor in the collapse of the Soviet Union.

Perhaps taken in isolation, any one of these factors would not have been enough to topple the mighty Soviet Union. But in combination, they were a recipe for political collapse. Glasnost led to more visibility of what really went on in the Soviet government as well as what was going on in the rest of the world. Disillusioned citizens became even more aware of how bleak their situation was in some ways, as glasnost allowed them to more freely express their displeasure. Perestroika and demokratizatsiya meant local and regional politics were no longer as tightly controlled by the CPSU as they had once been. Hovering over it all was the blanket of a crippled economy that showed no signs of strengthening. Factor in the ethnic fighting in numerous Soviet republics, and the splintering of the superpower was likely inevitable.

The fall of an entire nation cannot be attributed to just one face—or just three faces, in the case of Stalin, Khrushchev, and Gorbachev. Still, there's no doubt that the actions of all three leaders contributed to the collapse of the Soviet Union.

Prohibition, Soviet-Style

One of Gorbachev's first efforts at reform was to address the rampant alcoholism in the Soviet Union. Alcoholism has long been a major problem in the region, dating back at least to the Middle Ages. Parts of the region produce vodka, which naturally makes it cheap and relatively easy to get. Further, the Russian government (in its many forms over the years) has long supported its drinking citizens. Why? A simple answer: money. Alcohol and cigarettes are taxed, so the more liquor and tobacco people buy, the more money the government gets. In 2010, Russian finance minister Aleksei Kudrin stated that the best way citizens could help boost the Russian economy was by smoking and drinking more,

Alcoholism was one of the many problems in the Soviet Union that Gorbachev attempted to tackle.

yielding more taxes for the government. He further said that "those who drink are giving more to help solve social problems such as boosting demographics, developing other social services and upholding birth rates." This might be questionable logic, but his statement is quite an eye-opener when considering why alcoholism continues to be a major problem in Russia.

Gorbachev aimed to change this and mounted a strong anti-alcohol campaign shortly after he became the head of the Soviet Union. He raised taxes on alcohol and decreased state production of it. At first, his plan seemed to work. Worker productivity improved, family life improved as men were no longer out drinking and instead were at home, birth rates increased, and life expectancy increased. But eventually people began to make bootleg alcohol, and some even resorted to drinking poisonous alcoholic substances to get drunk, including antifreeze.

Further, the loss in tax revenue from alcohol was devastating to the Soviet economy—a loss of one hundred billion rubles, by some estimates. Gorbachev thought the loss in tax revenue would be offset by the increased worker productivity, but that did not turn out to be the case.

Fighting during the Cold War at times involved exposure to radiation or other chemicals, necessitating protective suits.

CHAPTER FOUR

Negotiation and Innovation

The Cold War essentially ended when the Soviet Union collapsed and its Communist government fell. The United States played a somewhat tangential role in these events. Much of what caused the fall of the Soviet Union was internal combustion—the fragile Soviet economy was further weakened by Gorbachev's attempts at political reform, ethnic conflicts in member republics of the Soviet Union, and increased transparency in government operations and in the media. But on the fringes of all this conflict was the United States. Its constant competition with the Soviet Union on weapons and space technology played a role in weakening the Soviet economy—perhaps the first major cracks in the superpower's foundation. Without the arms race and the space race, the outcome of the Soviet Union might have been quite different.

The Arms Race

In a sense, the arms race can be thought of as beginning in 1945, when President Harry Truman ordered atomic bombs to be dropped on Hiroshima and Nagasaki in Japan. Stalin, leader of the Soviet Union at the time, was determined not to fall behind the United States as a superpower, which would surely happen if the Soviet Union didn't possess similar weapons technology. Stalin ordered that the Soviet Union must immediately begin work on developing nuclear weapons, regardless of cost. By 1949, the Soviets had successfully tested their first nuclear device.

Not to be outdone, the United States began work on a hydrogen bomb in the early 1950s, detonating the first one in 1952, and not surprisingly, the Soviets began work on the same technology and detonated a similar bomb ten months later. However, the Soviet's bomb was not exactly the same as that being tested in the United States—rather, it was a similar thermonuclear device. The Soviets' first real hydrogen bomb was detonated in 1955.

Up to this point, the Soviets were just a hair behind the United States in weapons technology, but that was not always the case. When nuclear weapons were first developed, they were delivered by aircraft. B-29 bombers named the *Enola Gay* and *Bockscar* dropped the atomic bombs on Hiroshima and Nagasaki, respectively. But this delivery system was not particularly ideal—the planes could, in theory, be intercepted before reaching their targets, among other logistical problems. Missiles were considered a better delivery method, but missiles had limited distances over

The launch of *Sputnik* was a major step forward in the arms race.

which they could strike and were not always accurate in terms of reaching their intended target—that is, until *Sputnik*.

Sputnik was a satellite that the Soviets launched into orbit in October, 1957. It was launched on an R-7 ICBM. ICBMs were also considered a potential delivery device for nuclear weapons, and the Soviets' successful launch of *Sputnik* into orbit on an ICBM proved that the Soviets were capable of long-range delivery of nuclear weapons. The United States didn't develop a successful long-range ICBM until late in 1958.

Little Boy and the *Enola Gay*

Although two bombs were dropped on Japan near the end of World War II, the bombing of Hiroshima remains the more widely recognized of the two—perhaps because it was the first but also probably because the mortality was greater in Hiroshima. It was also in a flat area, whereas Nagasaki was in a hilly area.

A Boeing B-29 Superfortress bomber named the *Enola Gay* and piloted by Colonel Paul Tibbets dropped

The *Enola Gay* dropped the atomic bomb on Hiroshima.

the atomic bomb on Hiroshima on August 6, 1945. The bomb was nicknamed "Little Boy," and it caused mass destruction. Almost everything within a radius of one mile (1.6 kilometers) from where the bomb was dropped was destroyed. The roofs and walls on many buildings more than two miles (3.2 km) away were also destroyed. In total, sixty thousand of Hiroshima's ninety thousand structures were destroyed or severely damaged. The death toll immediately after the blast and within the first several months after totaled an estimated one hundred forty thousand people. (The bombing of Nagasaki resulted in another estimated eighty thousand deaths.)

Although the use of atomic weapons was undoubtedly devastating in terms of lives lost and structures destroyed, the United States' position on the matter was that far more lives would be lost if the war continued with more prolonged battles. The United States believed the bombs would end the war. And so, the *Enola Gay* and Little Boy are remembered both for their role in ending the war and for their role in causing mass devastation and loss of lives.

The Space Race

In some ways, the space race was very similar to the arms race. The Soviet Union and the United States both fought to remain on top. Which one could develop the best space technology? The space race was part of the arms race in that the technologies were similar—the technology developed for the space race could often be used in the arms race as well. For example, the same R-7 ICBM that launched *Sputnik* into orbit could, in theory, be used to deliver nuclear weapons.

However, the space race was also a matter of national pride. When he was head of the Soviet Union, Nikita Khrushchev said, "The *Sputniks* prove that Communism has won the competition between Communist and capitalist countries. The economy, science, culture and the creative genius of people in all areas of life develop better and faster under Communism." Meanwhile, United States president John F. Kennedy stated, "Everything we do ought to … be tied in to getting on to the Moon ahead of the Russians."

Kennedy initially expressed interest in joining forces with the Soviets where space technology was concerned, as he was concerned about the competition that could destroy both superpowers financially. In 1962, he suggested that "a cooperative Soviet-American effort in space science and exploration would emphasize the interests that must unite us, rather than those that always divide us." In a 1963 speech to the United Nations, he asked, "Why … should man's first flight to the moon be a matter of national competition? Why should the United States and the Soviet Union … become involved in immense duplications of research, construction, and expenditure?" Ultimately, though, it became clear that a collaboration between the two superpowers was not going to happen, and Kennedy resolved that the United States must put a man on the moon before the Soviets, even while acknowledging the immense expense involved, telling NASA administrator James Webb:

> *I do think we ought to get it, you know, really clear that … this is the top priority program of the agency and one of the two, except for defense, the top priority of the United States government. I think that's the position we ought to take. … Otherwise we shouldn't be spending this kind of money, because I'm not that interested in space. I think it's good. I think we ought to know about it. … But we're talking about fantastic expenditures which wreck our budget and all these other domestic programs, and the only justification for it, in my opinion … is because we hope to beat them and demonstrate that starting behind as we did, by a couple of years, by God, we passed them.*

This same financial issue plagued the Soviet Union—developing space technology was incredibly expensive, and the Soviets were already struggling to rebuild after the devastation of World War II.

The Soviet Union stayed ahead of the United States in space technology for a while, despite financial challenges. In addition to successfully launching the first satellite into orbit, they also sent the first human into space: Yuri Gagarin orbited the earth in the spacecraft *Vostok* in April 1961. However,

The United States jumped ahead in the space race when Neil Armstrong walked on the moon.

the United States won the race to the moon: Americans Neil Armstrong and Buzz Aldrin became the first men on the moon when *Apollo 11* landed on July 20, 1969.

This was a major feather in the United States' collective cap. After the debacle of the Bay of Pigs invasion and the drama created by the Cuban Missile Crisis, President Kennedy needed a way to rally the American public. Space was a new and exciting frontier, and the American public was keen to triumph over the Communist Soviet Union in some way. And so on September 12, 1962, when President Kennedy delivered an address at Rice University about the United States' plans to put a man on the moon, the American public was excited—the oft-quoted speech had the exact effect Kennedy had hoped for.

> *We set sail on this new sea because there is new knowledge to be gained, and new rights to be won, and they must be won and used for the progress of all people. For space science, like nuclear science and all technology, has no conscience of its own. Whether it will become a force for good or ill depends on man, and only if the United States occupies a position of preeminence can we help decide whether this new ocean will be a sea of peace or a new terrifying theater of war. … There is no strife, no prejudice, no national conflict in outer space as yet. Its hazards are hostile to us all. Its conquest deserves the best of all mankind, and its opportunity for peaceful cooperation may never come again. But why, some say, the moon? … We choose to go to the moon. We choose to go to the*

moon in this decade and do other things, not because they are easy, but because they are hard, because that goal will serve to organize and measure the best of our energies and skills, because that challenge is one that we are willing to accept, one we are unwilling to postpone, and one which we intend to win.

Rhetorically speaking, Kennedy's speech struck all the right notes. It reminded people of the threat of war and called on people's natural desire to triumph over the Soviet Union, which was seen as a constant, looming threat, particularly after the Cuban Missile Crisis.

A Tie Between Superpowers

It is virtually impossible to declare a winner in the arms race or the space race. The reality is that the Soviet Union and the United States traded the top spot back and forth as various developments unfolded. Ultimately, the nuclear arms were never deployed against each other, so there was no winner or loser. Both superpowers made major contributions to the discovery of new space technologies.

The one thing that is clear is that the arms race contributed to the continuing tensions between the two superpowers, and both the arms race and the space race contributed to the economic instability of the Soviet Union. The desire to keep up with or surpass the United States in technological development depleted funds that the Soviet Union didn't have and couldn't spare. When Gorbachev took leadership in 1985, the destroyed economy was a spreading crack in the foundation of the Soviet Union.

Modern Space Technology: The Hubble Space Telescope

Development in space technology continues today, but not at the same fevered pace as during the Cold War. Despite the slower pace, people have not lost their interest in space simply because the Cold War has ended. In fact, one of the biggest developments in space technology took place near the very end of the Cold War, and it continues to be used today: the Hubble telescope.

The Hubble space telescope was launched into orbit in 1990 and has been updated over the years since. It has instruments and cameras that allow scientists to capture images of deep space they would not otherwise be able to obtain. The Hubble's technologies have allowed scientists to make discoveries about **quasars, dark energy**, and life cycles of galaxies. They have also enabled scientists to determine a more accurate date for the universe's origin and a more accurate rate of expansion for the universe.

The Hubble is solar-powered and can be serviced in space by astronauts, so it has remained in orbit since its launch in 1990, and it could potentially remain in orbit until as late as 2040.

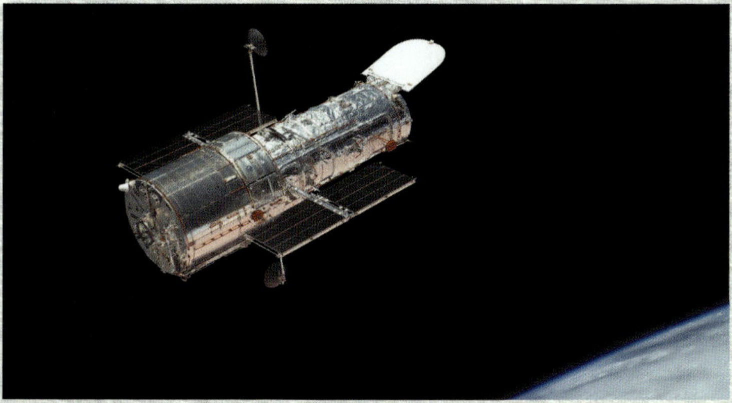

The Hubble telescope was launched near the very end of the Cold War.

Lithuanians celebrated the vote for independence from the Soviet Union in 1991.

CHAPTER FIVE

The Legacy of the Collapse of Communism and the Breakup of the Soviet Union

While there is no firm end date to the Cold War, just as there is no absolute start date, many historians agree that the collapse of the Soviet Union marked the end of the Cold War. The Cold War was based on two superpowers jockeying for the top spot, and when one of those superpowers fell, there was suddenly no more jockeying required. This brought immense relief to many people who had lived under the shadow of the Cold War, but it also left a lasting legacy.

Post–Cold War Life in the United States

Immediately after the Cold War, Americans began to emerge from the shell of fear that had encased them for decades. The Soviet Union had been the United States' biggest threat for decades. American soldiers fought in proxy wars (Korea and Vietnam) in large part to prevent the spread of Communism that would make the Soviet Union more powerful. Americans lived in fear during times when nuclear war seemed possible, such as during the Cuban Missile Crisis. Domestically, they had lived under Senator Joseph McCarthy's **Red Scare**, in which innocent Americans were accused of Communism in a modern-day witch hunt.

When the Cold War ended, the United States was long past the Red Scare, but the fear of Communism still lingered. In some ways, the fall of the Soviet Union meant the end of that fear. While China is still a Communist nation, it is not the superpower that the Soviet Union was. (Some argue that China is technically a capitalist nation with Communist elements; however, the Communist Party of China is the sole governing party, which makes it essentially a Communist nation.) United States relations with China have generally been fairly stable. There have been periods of instability, but on the whole, international relations between the two countries have been largely stable, unlike the tense relations that existed between the United States and the Soviet Union. Cuba, too, is still under Communist rule, but on its own, Cuba has not been a major threat to United States security. (When the Soviets placed nuclear weapons in Cuba, that was a whole other story. But Cuba on its own has not been a particular threat even though relations have long been strained between the two countries.)

Certainly there are other Communist countries—in fact, many of the countries that made up the Soviet Union are currently under Communist governments. After all, the fall of the Soviet Union did not mean the fall of Communism. But, like Cuba, many of these countries do not pose a significant threat to United States security.

But fears in the United States have simply shifted. Americans no longer worry about the threat of a Communist superpower, but they do worry about the threat of militant and radical terrorist groups and smaller nations like North Korea and Iran that have the potential to develop nuclear weapons and that do not consider the United States an ally. Al-Qaeda was a concern in the 1990s and 2000s, and more recently the Islamic State (ISIS and other splinter groups) poses a threat to American national security. These terrorist groups are not as large in number as the Soviet Union, but their unpredictability and access to devastating weapons has created a similar looming threat over American national security.

Russia comprised the largest portion of the Soviet Union, and it is now the largest and most powerful country among the countries that formerly made up the Soviet Union. United States relations with Russia have been stable but uneasy over recent years. The two countries are not outright at odds with one another, but calling them allies might be a bit of an overstatement. There have been a number of tense exchanges between the United States government and the Russian government under President Vladimir Putin in recent years. In addition, the 2016 United States presidential election further exposed the tense nature of the relationship between the two nations. Security officials in the United States accused Russia of **cyber-hacking** and leaking information that could create a bias in the United States presidential

The Egyptian army carried out airstrikes against ISIS targets in Libya in early 2015.

election. Specifically, United States security officials felt that Russia was trying to influence the election in Republican candidate Donald Trump's favor. Whether that was really the case, no one knows; however, it certainly created additional tension during the election.

Since Trump did end up winning the 2016 election, the future of United States relations with Russia remains to be seen as of this writing. During Trump's campaign, he expressed a desire to improve United States relations with Russia, saying at a rally in Iowa in early 2016, "Wouldn't

Russian president Putin and US president Obama had a rather tense working relationship.

it be nice if we actually got along with Russia and China and all these countries? … So that when we have an ISIS threat and we have these threats they can actually spend money and put money into things and knock the hell out of them also—it's not always us, the policemen of the world." Putin, whose relationship with President Barack Obama had been tense, has lavishly praised Trump, saying, "He is a very colorful and talented man, no doubt about that. … He says that he wants to move to another level of relations, to a deeper level of relations with Russia. How can we not welcome that? Of course we welcome it." What happens with relations between the United States and Russia over the course of Trump's presidency remains to be seen as well as what effect that will have on the American public.

Post–Cold War Life in the Former Soviet States

The former Soviet republics are many, and the effects they experienced after the Cold War ended are varied. Some are still fighting internal ethnic battles, while others have settled into a period of peace. Economically, though, there were some fairly serious repercussions from the Cold War.

Russia, the largest of the former Soviet republics, experienced large-scale unemployment because many Russians had been employed in military or industrial jobs during the Cold War, and military spending was drastically cut after the Cold War ended.

Russia also attempted economic reforms immediately after the Cold War that resulted in a tremendous economic

Poverty was a way of life for many in the Soviet Union when it collapsed.

recession and negatively impacted the standard of living for many Russians. The economy has experienced some regrowth in the years since, but immediately after the Cold War, the recession was deep and devastating.

Although the republics that made up the Soviet Union are no longer controlled under one Communist government, some of the republics do still share a symbolic link. In late

1991, the Commonwealth of Independent States (CIS) was founded. The CIS does not hold full power over the states, like the Soviet government had, but it holds some power in coordinating matters of trade, finance, security, and legislation. The CIS is made up of nine former Soviet republics (Armenia, Azerbaijan, Belarus, Kazakhstan, Kyrgyzstan, Moldova, Russia, Tajikistan, and Uzbekistan) and two associate members (Ukraine and Turkmenistan). Georgia was once part of the CIS but withdrew its membership in 2008 due to the Russo-Georgian War.

The Cold War in Contemporary Life

To those born near the end of or after the Cold War, it is merely another marker in history. But a huge segment of the current population was alive during the Cold War, and for many it is almost surreal to think of the end of that long era. For decades, the Soviet Union was the enemy of the United States, and American citizens lived under the constant, looming threat that if tensions grew too great between the two superpowers, nuclear war could break out.

East and West Germany were essentially two different countries. It was just a fact. American citizens could—and did—travel freely to West Germany and other Western European countries, but few ventured behind the **Iron Curtain**. When they did, they often had stories about the incredible difference in living conditions between the United States and Communist countries. East Germans and Russians appeared regularly at the Olympics and often dominated in particular sports, such as ice-skating,

The Cold War in Popular Culture

One legacy of the Cold War is that it continues to figure as a subject in art, film, and literature. So rich is the history of the decades of the Cold War that it is likely to remain a topic of interest for filmmakers and authors for years to come. Some of the most popular films to depict aspects of the Cold War include *North by Northwest* (1959), an Alfred Hitchcock spy thriller starring Cary Grant; *The Manchurian Candidate* (1962), starring Frank Sinatra as the brainwashed son of a political family who goes on to become an assassin; *Dr.*

Chancellor of Germany Angela Merkel (*center*) speaks to director Steven Spielberg (*left*) and actor Tom Hanks (*right*) in Berlin, Germany, on the set of the movie *Bridge of Spies*, which tells the story of Cold War prisoner exchange.

Strangelove or How I Learned to Stop Worrying and Love the Bomb (1964), a Stanley Kubrick satire on the public's fears about the Cold War; *The Hunt for Red October*, a political thriller released near the tail end of the Cold War; and more recently, *Bridge of Spies* (2015), the story of Cold War prisoner exchange.

In literature, many novelists have used the Cold War as a backdrop. Ian Fleming wrote the fifth book in his James Bond series of books, *From Russia, With Love* (1957), about assassination attempts by a Soviet counterintelligence agency. Richard Condon's *The Manchurian Candidate* (1959) was a well-regarded novel before being made into a successful film. Novelist John le Carré set *The Spy Who Came in From the Cold* (1963) against the backdrop of the Cold War. E. L. Doctorow's *The Book of Daniel* (1971) is a fictionalized account of Ethel and Julius Rosenberg, American Communists who were executed for sharing secrets about the atomic bomb with the Soviets. Contemporary authors Ian McEwan and Don DeLillo set *The Innocent* (1990) and *Underworld* (1997), respectively, in the Cold War era.

The physical destruction of the Berlin Wall described the figurative rebuilding of the divided city and country.

hockey, and gymnastics, but otherwise stayed behind the Iron Curtain. It was a reality that few Americans expected would ever really change.

But when the Soviet Union fell, things did begin to change. American citizens began to travel to countries like Poland, Romania, and even Russia, which all had previously rarely been destinations. Citizens from these former republics also gained freedoms they hadn't had before either.

Certainly, there are still tensions between the United States and some of the former republics of the Soviet Union. But post–Cold War relations are very different from what many Americans ever thought they would see.

Chronology

1924 Stalin takes leadership of the Soviet Union.

1936–1938 Stalin's Great Purge results in the death or exile of millions.

1945 Yalta and Potsdam summits occur.

1948 The Marshall Plan goes into effect.

1948–1949 The Berlin blockade occurs, in which the Soviet Union attempts to block the Allies from getting supplies to the parts of Berlin under Allied control.

1949 Soviet Union detonates its first atomic device, four years after the United States bombed Hiroshima and Nagasaki.

1950–1953 The Korean War, a proxy war of the Cold War, takes place.

1953 Joseph Stalin dies.

1955–1975 The Vietnam War, a proxy war of the Cold War, takes place.

1957 The Soviet Union launches *Sputnik*.

1958	Nikita Khrushchev assumes leadership over the Soviet Union.
1961	President John F. Kennedy takes office.
1962	The Cuban Missile Crisis takes place.
1969	Neil Armstrong and Buzz Aldrin become the first humans on the moon.
1981	President Ronald Reagan takes office.
1985	Mikhail Gorbachev takes leadership of the Soviet Union and begins campaigns of perestroika and glasnost.
1989	Revolutions in central and Eastern Europe begin to fracture Soviet rule over the area.
1990	The Communist Party of the Soviet Union (CPSU) votes to end one-party rule in the Soviet Union.
1991	The Congress of People's Deputies votes to dissolve the Soviet Union. Gorbachev resigns, effectively ending the Cold War.
2016	Fidel Castro dies at the age of ninety.

Glossary

Bolsheviks Members of the Russian Social Democratic Labour Party, a Marxist group that eventually became the Communist Party of the Soviet Union (CPSU).

censorship The suppression of free speech and information that might be considered objectionable or politically incorrect.

command economy An economic system in which the central government controls production, investment, pricing, and income decisions.

coup d'état Overthrow of the government by members of the military or others within the government.

cult of personality A culture in which a person uses mass media or propaganda to build up an idealized persona.

cyber-hacking Exploiting the weaknesses in a computer system to uncover classified or confidential material.

dark energy A form of energy thought to permeate all of space.

Great Purge A campaign of political repression under Stalin's rule that sought to purge from the Communist Party any members who were thought to be enemies of the state.

gross domestic product The measure of the market value of goods and services produced over a specified period of time.

gulag Forced labor camps in the Soviet Union during thc years Stalin was in power.

intercontinental ballistic missile (ICBM) A guided missile with a range of about 3,400 miles (5,472 kilometers) that is generally used for delivering nuclear weapons.

Iron Curtain The figurative barrier between the Eastern Bloc and the Western Bloc during the Cold War.

Marxist Follower of the Marxist school of Communism, which is derived from the work of philosophers Karl Marx and Friedrich Engels.

nationalist A member of a political organization promoting a country's political independence.

Politburo The main policymaking body for the Communist Party of the Soviet Union.

quasar Massive celestial objects that emit large amounts of energy.

Red Army The army and air force of the Soviet Union.

Red Scare The fear of a potential rise of Communism. The United States experienced a Red Scare due to the ideas of Senator Joseph McCarthy.

seminary A school that educates students in theology.

sovereign Independent and without outside interference.

Bibliography

DeGroot, Gerard J. *Dark Side of the Moon: The Magnificent Madness of the American Lunar Quest*. New York: New York University Press, 2006.

Ellman, Michael, and S. Maksudov. "Soviet Deaths in the Great Patriotic War: A Note." *Europe-Asia Studies* 46 (1994): 671–680.

Fedun, Stan. "How Alcohol Conquered Russia." *The Atlantic*, September 25, 2013. http://www.theatlantic.com/international/archive/2013/09/how-alcohol-conquered-russia/279965/.

Khrushchev, Nikita. *Memoirs of Nikita Khrushchev, Volume 2: Reformer*. University Park, PA: Pennsylvania State University Press, 2006.

Oliphant, Roland. "The Awkward Moment When Barack Obama and Vladimir Putin Met at the UN General Assembly." *The Telegraph*, September 29, 2015. http://www.telegraph.co.uk/news/worldnews/vladimir-putin/11898993/The-awkward-moment-when-

Barack-Obama-and-Vladimir-Putin-met-at-the-UN-General-Assembly.html.

Schmemann, Serge. "END OF THE SOVIET UNION: The Soviet State, Born of a Dream, Dies." *The New York Times*, December 26, 1991. http://www.nytimes.com/1991/12/26/world/end-of-the-soviet-union-the-soviet-state-born-of-a-dream-dies.html?pagewanted=all.

Schrad, Mark Lawrence. "Moscow's Drinking Problem." *The New York Times*, April 16, 2011. http://www.nytimes.com/2011/04/17/opinion/17Schrad.html?_r=0.

Taliaferro, Jeffrey W. *Balancing Risks: Great Power Intervention in the Periphery*. Ithaca, NY: Cornell University Press, 2004.

Taubman, Philip. "Gorbachev Says Ethnic Unrest Could Destroy Restructuring Effort." *The New York Times*, November 28, 1988. http://www.nytimes.com/1988/11/28/world/gorbachev-says-ethnic-unrest-could-destroy-restructuring-effort.html.

Volkogonov, Dmitri. *Stalin: Triumph and Tragedy*. New York: Grove Press, 1991.

Waldman, Michael. *My Fellow Americans: The Most Important Speeches of America's Presidents, from George Washington to Barack Obama*. Naperville, IL: Sourcebooks MediaFusion, 2010.

Waugh, Steven. *Essential Modern World History*. Oxford: Oxford University Press, 2014.

Widmer, Ted. *Listening In: The Secret White House Recordings of John F. Kennedy*. New York: Hyperion Books, 2012.

Further Information

Books

Figes, Orlando. *Revolutionary Russia 1891–1991: A History*. New York: Metropolitan Books, 2014.

Marcovitz, Hal. *Cause & Effect: The Fall of the Soviet Union*. San Diego: ReferencePoint Press, 2015.

Plokhy, Serhii. *The Last Empire: The Final Days of the Soviet Union*. New York: Basic Books, 2015.

Wilson, James Graham. *The Triumph of Improvisation: Gorbachev's Adaptability, Reagan's Engagement, and the End of the Cold War*. Ithaca, NY: Cornell University Press, 2015.

Websites

The Cold War Museum

http://www.coldwar.org

This website provides links to the major events, conflicts, and faces of the Cold War.

Marxists International Archive

http://www.marxists.org

Marxism is a school of Communism, and this website provides information on the history of Communism, ideas espoused by Communist leaders, and various archived materials on Communism.

Office of the Historian

https://history.state.gov/milestones/1989-1992/collapse-soviet-union

This website features various resources on the collapse of the Soviet Union that are all archived by professional historians.

Royal Air Force Museum

http://www.nationalcoldwarexhibition.org

The Royal Air Force Museum hosts the National Cold War Exhibition, and the website is full of information about Cold War events.

Videos

The Cold War: The Complete Series

https://www.youtube.com/playlist?list=PL3H6z037pboGWTxs3xGP7HRGrQ5dOQdGc

This series from the BBC features various events of Cold War history with footage of the most significant people and places from the Cold War.

The End of the USSR

https://www.youtube.com/watch?v=0g6arFbKZ60

This documentary from the Discovery Channel explores the collapse of the Soviet Union with interview footage of Mikhail Gorbachev.

Index

Page numbers in **boldface** are illustrations. Entries in **boldface** are glossary terms.

About the Author

Cathleen Small is an editor and author who has written more than two dozen books for students in grades three through twelve. Having been born in the early 1970s, she remembers well the reign of Mikhail Gorbachev, the Soviet reforms, and the ultimate fall of the Soviet Union. Cathleen lives in the San Francisco Bay Area. When she is not writing or editing, she enjoys traveling and spending time with her husband and two young sons.